This book goes to my youngest yet greatest inspirations, Annabella and Felix.
Remember "Every big dream starts with a little dream
and every little dream starts at Love."

Genuinely yours,
Auntie Lau – xoxo

Original title: It starts at love

Written by Laura Vallverdu
Edited by Laura Vallverdu & Augie Haas
Illustrations by Marta Contel
Copyright © 2021, Laura Vallverdu
First edition: 2021

For more information, address: tennisbetweenlines@gmail.com

It starts at love

Written by Laura Vallverdu - Illustrated by Marta Contel

*M*eet Laura – though her friends and family
called her Little Lau.

She was always full of energy and LOVED to play outside.

Her favorite person in the whole wide world
was her big brother Daniel.

Dani and Little Lau were best friends and always had
so much fun playing sports together!

Dani swings; Little Lau catches.
Dani dribbles; Little Lau defends.
Dani kicks; Little Lau blocks.
Dani swims; Little Lau starts the clock.
And so it goes...

One day, the whole family was watching Dani win his first swim competition.
"Go Dani, gooo" – they cheered.

Little Lau in the crowd, closed her eyes super hard
and wished to one day be in a competition, just like Dani.

After Dani was done swimming, Little Lau went on a walk around the club.
To her surprise, every step she took,
distant cheering was getting louder and louder.

"WOO" "CLAP" "CLAP" "YEAAAA" "LETS GOOO"!!

*F*ull of energy, Little Lau sprinted
as fast as she could.

Out of breath, she found herself
at the tennis courts to see a sight her eyes
had never ever seen before!

Back and forth the little yellow ball went.
Over the net, into the net,
through the air at a million miles an hour!
How could this be?!?

"What's going on here?"
Little Lau asked someone in the crowd.

They replied,
"This is tennis, the best sport in the world!!!".

Little Lau watched and watched and watched alllllll afternoon, until the sun went down.

"That's it, this is what I want".

Little Lau decided to play tennis in front of her family and friends. She wanted to be a tennis champion one day.

That night, Little Lau could barely sleep.
She dreamt of little yellow balls going side to side.
Racquets swinging back and forth.
People clapping left and right.

SOOO EXCITING!!

The next morning, Little Lau couldn't contain herself.
She kept swinging her imaginary racquet back and forth
running all around the house.
Her parents asked her what she was doing.

She replied
"I am playing tennis!" It is soooooo awesome!
Will you get me a real racquet?"
Please please please please!

Little Lau's mom and dad understood
how excited she was about playing tennis and decided
to buy her first racquet for Christmas that year.

"THANK YOU."

"THANK YOU."

"THANK YOU."

THANK YOU,"

"I cannot wait for my first lesson!!!"

"THANK YOU,"

"THANK YOU."

Little Lau got to her first lesson, took a big swing and "whoops" she missed the ball over and over again.

Little Lau kept practicing, she wanted to play like the kids in the tournament.

Mom and Dad asked after the lesson
"*How did it go?*"

Little Lau said
"*It's not as easy as I thought*"

They both smiled and told her
"*Remember, any dream starts
with loving what you do*"

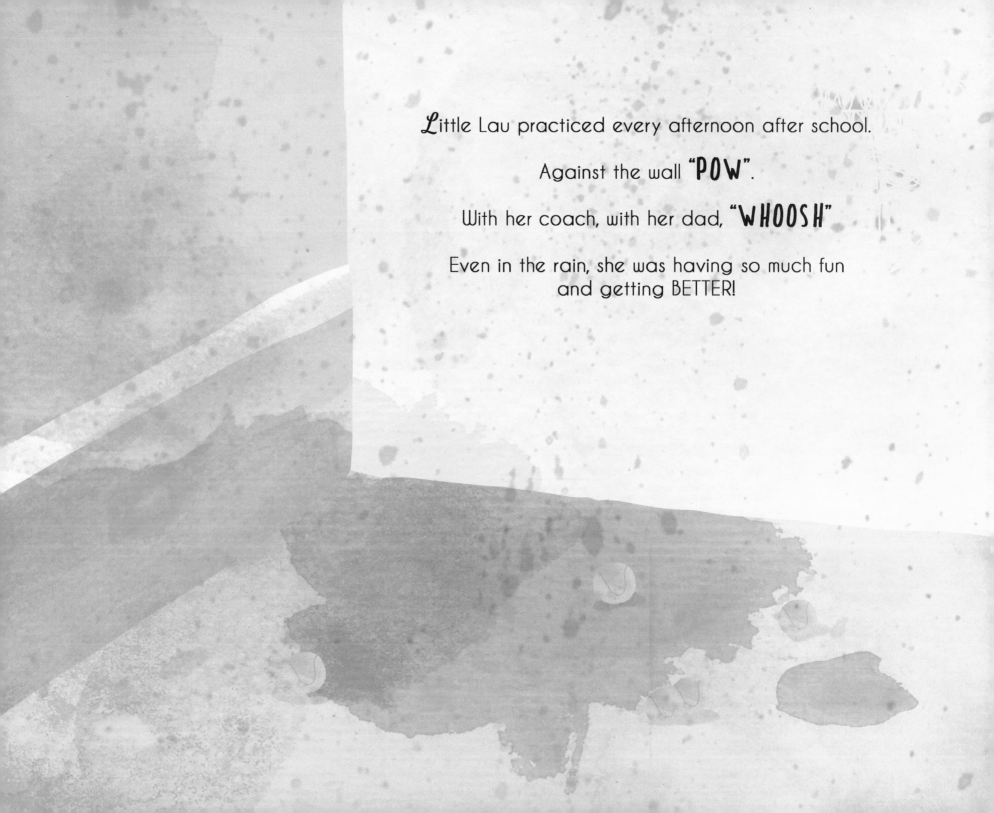

Little Lau practiced every afternoon after school.

Against the wall "**POW**".

With her coach, with her dad, "**WHOOSH**"

Even in the rain, she was having so much fun
and getting BETTER!

Finally, Little Lau practiced so much,
her coach signed her up for her very first tournament.

Her family and friends were all super happy.

They packed their coolers with snacks
and went to watch Little Lau's first tournament together.

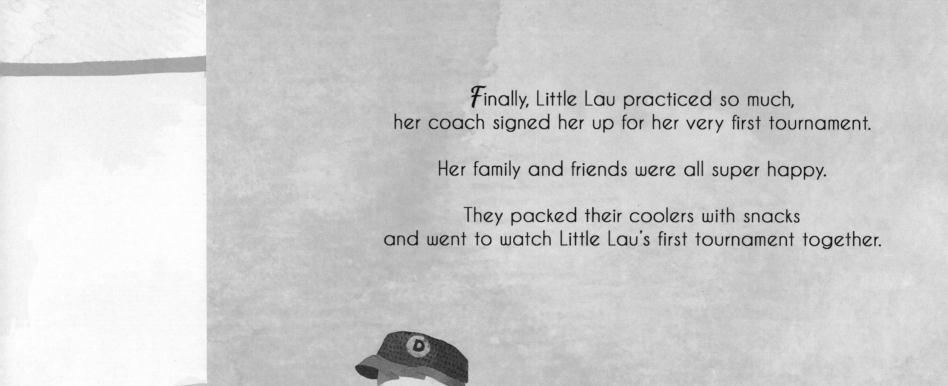

But there was a minor problem that day...
everyone was smiling, except Little Lau.
Her big brother Dani went to see her and asked:

"what's going on?"

"I am nervous, and I don't know why?"

Dani put his arm around Little Lau and said

"Today is a celebration... just remember how much
you love tennis and how hard you practiced.

Just imagine you are playing against me
and I am sure you'll have a lot of fun"

Little Lau finally smiled, gave her big
brother a high five and said,

"You are right, thank you".

She was now ready to go out and play
in front of her family and friends.

"CLAP" "CLAP" "WELL DONE" "WOOO"
Her family and friends were so happy and proud of her.
Little Lau loved her first tennis tournament.
She decided to never ever stop practicing.

She learned that every dream starts
with hard work, and lots of practice.

BUT all that matters, is that you LOVE what you do,
and you always SHARE it with friends and family.